SUMMER CAMP

Summer Camp is published by Stone Arch Books,
A Capstone Imprint
1710 Roe Crest Drive
North Mankato, Minnesota 56003

Library of Congress Cataloging-in-Publication Data
Names: Brandes, Wendy L., 1965- author. | Lorenzet, Eleonora,
    illustrator.
Title: Claire's cursed camping trip / by Wendy L. Brandes;
    [illustrator, Eleonora Lorenzet].
Description: North Mankato, Minnesota: Stone Arch books, an
    imprint of Capstone Press, [2017] | Series: Summer camp |
    Summary: Twelve-year-old Claire is at summer camp with her
    friends, just as they have been doing for the past four years, but
    when Emily and Nina get into a fight, Claire finds herself in the
    middle and mad at both of them—right before the raft trip and
    forest hike that will require all their cooperation.
Identifiers: LCCN 2016020946 | ISBN 9781496526007 (library
    binding) | ISBN 9781496527134 (pbk.) | ISBN 9781496527172
    (ebook (pdf))
Subjects: LCSH: Camps—Juvenile fiction. | Camping—Juvenile
    fiction. | Hiking—Juvenile fiction. | Best friends—Juvenile
    fiction. | Friendship—Juvenile fiction. | CYAC: Camps—Fiction.
    | Camping—Fiction. | Hiking—Fiction. | Best friends—Fiction. |
    Friendship—Fiction.
Classification: LCC PZ7.1.B7515 Cl 2017 | DDC 813.6 [Fic]—dc23
LC record available at https://lccn.loc.gov/2016020946

Illustrated by Eleonora Lorenzet

Printed and bound in the USA
009661CGF16

>>>— SUMMER CAMP —→

CLAIRE'S CURSED
CAMPING TRIP

BY WENDY L. BRANDES

STONE ARCH BOOKS
a capstone imprint

FIND YOUR ADVENTURE AT

CAMP MON MON LAKE!

Camp Mon Mon Lake, an all-girls sleepaway camp in Maine, has it all! Girls return year after year for friendship, challenges, and fun. And every year, they take home memories of a magical summer filled with the warmth of a summer family.

We group our campers according to age. Each group is assigned a different bird name—and there are A LOT of different birds up here! Our youngest group is the Hummingbirds (ages 7–8) and our oldest group is the Condors, also known as the Seniors (ages 14–15). In between we have Blue Jays, Robins, and Songbirds.

At Mon Mon Lake, we fill the weeks with singing, spirit, activity, and group bonding. No matter what your interests are, we have an activity for you!

MON MON'S SUMMER ACTIVITIES

LAND SPORTS

ARCHERY
BASKETBALL
CLIMBING WALL
FIELD HOCKEY
GYMNASTICS
LACROSSE
RIDING
SOCCER
SOFTBALL
TENNIS
VOLLEYBALL
YOGA

WATER SPORTS

CANOEING
KAYAKING
SAILING
SWIMMING
WATERSKIING

THE ARTS

DANCE
DRAMA
DRAWING
PAINTING
POTTERY

WHAT CAMPERS ARE SAYING:

"I didn't want to come to camp at all, but that's before I met my bunkmates. The girls at Camp Mon Mon make the best friends."
— MJ, a new camper

"I love the swimming, the intercamp games, and all the fun in the bunk—especially pranking our counselors!"
— Emily, a four-year camp veteran

"I love the group shows. Being onstage in front of the entire camp—and the boys' camp next door—is amazing! No place is more fun than Camp Mon Mon Lake!"
— Nina, a Blue Jay (age 13)

"The camp trips are my favorite part about camp. What could be better than hiking and camping out with your best friends?"
— Claire, award winner for Best Outdoorswoman

CHAPTER 1

Three. Not the best number. Two is a pair. Best friends come in twos. And three? I guess three is a triangle or three of a kind. Best friends can come in threes too, I guess. But sometimes it's *two* plus *one*, with the one hanging by itself. Sometimes that's me—I'm the *one* left alone.

This is my fifth summer at Camp Mon Mon Lake, and I have two best friends, Emily and Nina. We're all totally tight. Ask them who their best friends are, and they'll say each other and me. But every once in a while, three doesn't work.

I don't know if Nina and Emily ever feel like they're on the outside, but I sometimes do. When that happens, it's like they have an unspoken language that doesn't exactly include me.

I hate feeling insecure. I try to think of myself as being true to who I am, following my own path. I usually don't care if I'm the odd one out. But when we have to break into twos for whatever reason, I sometimes worry that I'm the one who's going to be looking for a partner. And I hate that feeling.

CHAPTER 2

"Why are you writing a camping guide?" MJ, one of the two new campers in my bunk, asked as we checked the gear we were bringing on the rafting trip.

"It's not a guide, exactly. Arlene—you know, the head of camp trips—asked me if I could take some notes on this year's Blue Jay group trip since it's our first time going whitewater rafting. She wants to have something on hand for next year. So I'm just going to jot down notes about how we prep and what goes on at the campsite."

"That's cool. Everyone says that you are the best when it comes to outdoor stuff," MJ replied.

"Well, I have the most outdoor badges from our group. And I definitely love camping. I feel like I'm at my best when I'm in the wilderness." I smiled. "Now help me check everyone's pack for flashlights."

We were halfway through our bunk's packs when Emily burst in. "What are you guys doing?" she asked.

"Checking everyone's packs to make sure we all have flashlights, water bottles, first aid kits, granola bars—" I said.

"Granola! Now there's a good nickname for you, our vegan goddess," Emily said to me.

I rolled my eyes. "Do you really think that Granola is a good nickname?" I asked. "You know that if you make fun of a vegan, animal rights groups will come after you, right?"

MJ giggled.

"What about Grans? That's a good nickname. You've got to admit it," Emily said.

I shook my head. "Sounds like a grandma. I'll pass. Just Claire is fine."

"Nola?" Emily asked.

"Doesn't a nickname just sort of have to happen organically?" MJ said.

"Yeah, MJ. I agree," I said. "Emily's been trying to come up with the perfect nickname for me for five years, and so far, nothing's caught on."

Emily stuck her tongue out at me. "I'm going to get it this year. Nola. It's such a cool nickname."

"Totally forced," I said.

"Remember last year, I almost got GTS to stick," Emily said.

"What's GTS?" MJ asked.

"Goody Two Shoes," Emily said with a mischievous grin on her face.

"Yeah, that wasn't *too* forced either," I said, rolling my eyes again.

"Claire isn't a GTS," MJ said.

"Thank you!" I slung my arm around MJ. "Now, *this* is a true friend."

"I'll keep working on a better nickname. Don't worry, I'll come up with the perfect one before camp's over," Emily said.

"I know you will, Em," I said, certain she wouldn't stop trying.

I didn't mind the nicknames, but at the same time, they kind of bugged me. My mom once told me that in France there's a word for something that's ugly, but at the same time, beautiful.

I sometimes wished there was a word for liking being teased about something, but also having it annoy you a little bit. It would be a word that combined being a good sport and getting a little tired of it. *Sportsausted.*

Or maybe *tolerannoy*. The nickname thing definitely *tolerannoyed* me.

All three of us continued to go through the packs and checked off everything on our list. I grabbed a notebook and wrote: *RAFTING TRIP TIP #1: Check your equipment. Make sure you have everything you need and that it's all in good working condition.*

"What are you writing?" Emily asked.

"The Blue Jay's Guide to Whitewater Rafting," I replied. "I'm up to the part where I tell everyone to check their equipment."

"So are you going to make sure everyone brings a life preserver and a lucky penny?" Emily asked with a big grin.

I giggled. "Hopefully, we won't need either." I put down my notebook. "I gotta go to the nurse before we finish packing for the trip," I said. "Gotta get every allergy medication under the sun."

"Yeah, Nola. We can't have you puffing up like you did during the Color War. That was crazy," Emily said.

I ignored the nickname and said, "I was really disappointed that I didn't get to row in the Wacky Relay—all because of my stupid allergies."

"Well, you're gonna get to row on our trip to Mount Wanscopic. I'm counting on you to do the heavy lifting," Emily replied.

"Aye, aye. As long as you remember I'm the captain," I said.

"Yes, yes. Captain Nola," said Emily as she gave me a big salute.

"Argh!" I exclaimed, gathering my stuff to go. She just wouldn't let up!

"I'll come with you. I have to go take care of Duck," MJ said.

"Duck? We don't have ducks at camp," I said.

"My horse—Duck. The gray mare," she said.

MJ and I headed out of the bunk and walked toward the infirmary and the stables.

"Are you going to be in a raft with Emily and Nina?" she asked. "'Cause Zoe and I were going to ask you to come in ours."

"That's so sweet of you. I guess Nina, Emily, and I have always been together, so I just assumed that we'd stay in the same raft. Who knows, though? This year they might just assign us."

"I absolutely hate having to worry about finding partners. I'd rather that counselors just put us in groups," MJ said.

"Me too."

"But our bunk is so chill," MJ added. "You could switch anyone in our bunk around, and we'd all be happy to be buddied up."

"True," I said. And it was. Even though I got hung up on who was going to be the odd person out, our bunk was awesome. The two newbies, Zoe and MJ, were super cool. We'd had a lot of good times already.

"Are you going to be okay on the trip?" MJ asked. "With your allergies, I mean."

"After I blew up like a giant pool float before the Wacky Relay, the nurse wants me to be super careful. And Astrid and Susannah, our overprotective counselors, want me to bring a whole over-the-counter pharmacy with me on our camping trip."

"I don't blame them. That whole thing when you got so swollen? That was totally weird. I was super worried," MJ said.

"I definitely don't want to let anything wreck our camping trip. It's probably my favorite thing at camp," I said.

"Well, I'll see you back at the bunk, after I clean Duck's stall. Later," MJ said and continued walking down the path.

I opened the door to the infirmary and was blasted by cool, refreshing air. Ahh, it pays to be sick sometimes!

Even though camp had been nearly perfect so far, I was sure the camping trip would be the highlight of the summer. Okay, so maybe "perfect" was a stretch. MJ and Zoe got into a fight the first week or so because Zoe's dad is famous and MJ knew it and Zoe worried nobody liked her for her. It all worked out, but not before there was drama.

Then we decided to prank Susannah, our counselor, for being way too strict. She *wigged out* when we put a water balloon under her pillow. But she made up with everyone. Also, Emily told everyone that her parents were arguing and maybe on the way to a divorce. It's hard to see Emily, who is the toughest in our bunk, getting so upset.

After that, I got the lead in *Wicked* while Nina got a smaller part, even though she had always been the star in our group shows. I was worried it would hurt our friendship, plus I had stage fright. I actually had an attack of hiccups right before the curtain went up. Hiccups. For real.

But Nina was great. She really helped me get through all the stuff I was afraid of, including hiccups. And I have to admit that I loved—L-O-V-E-D—being in the play. I'm usually at my best—my most confident—when I'm outdoors. Nature is my thing. But being a star onstage for the first time? It was awesome.

And tomorrow our whole Blue Jays group is going to ride the rapids—or at least whatever whitewater there is in southern Maine. We'll go on to camp out for two nights at the Wanscopic campsite. Astrid, our counselor, told us that some of the boys from Eagle Rock might meet up with us at some point during our trip. I'd be psyched if they did, because I like a bunch of the boys I've met at this year's camp events with Eagle Rock.

Anyway, after visiting the nurse, who gave me lots of instructions and made sure I understood what meds I should carry with me at all times and which the counselors would have, I returned to our bunk. I was on the porch about to open the door when I heard screaming. I rushed in just in time to hear Nina yell, "I can't believe you would do that to me! I totally can't believe it!"

CHAPTER 3

Nina was screaming at Emily. They have N-E-V-E-R had a fight before. Two-thirds of our threesome was blowing up.

I charged into the middle of the bunk. "Quiet!" I shouted. But they didn't stop. They were both yelling at once. I tried to do one of those taxi whistles, but all that came out was a sad little squeak. Finally, I held up my hand and screamed, "Quit it!"

Thankfully, they both finally noticed me, and each stopped shouting.

"*What* is going on?" I asked, looking from one to the other. Neither said anything.

Finally, Emily said, "Tell her if you want."

Nina sniffed loudly. "You just didn't have to be so mean about it." She lifted the bottom of her T-shirt to her face and dried her eyes.

"Mean about what?" I asked. "What is going on with you two?"

"Nina overheard me saying that I didn't really want her in our raft," Emily answered.

I stared at Emily. "What are you talking about? Of course we're all rafting together," I said. "That's what we've always done."

"I know that's what we've done before, but I kind of want to switch things up this year. Nothing against her," Emily said as if Nina wasn't even there.

Nina started crying. I walked over to her and put my arm on her back. "I want to be with you, Neens."

"So you're taking *her* side?" Emily asked.

"What side? What are you even talking about?" I asked. "I was with you checking our packs fifteen minutes ago, and you didn't say anything at all. What exactly is going on?"

"What's going on is the whole Nina-and-Zac thing," Emily said. "I just don't know how things are supposed to be the same when she's suddenly my brother's best friend. And it all started with them going behind my back and stuff."

"I knew that's what this was about. I knew it!" Nina said. "Emily, you and I are friends. And Zac and I are friends. So what? Why do you have to turn it into an 'Emily Big Deal'?"

I stood up. "Listen, you guys. You are best friends. Is any of this worth getting so mad? It can't be."

"I'm not doing anything. I just—" Emily stopped. "I just—" She stopped again. Then she just started crying.

Panic time. Emily and Nina both crying? A collapsing triangle is scary! Plus, it was bizarre to see Emily crying. Until her big announcement about her parents, I didn't think she even knew how to cry.

"Guys, guys, guys," I said. "You don't want to be mad at each other. You don't. And I don't want to be the only sane one here."

They laughed.

"Seriously. I don't," I repeated. "So, take a breath. Now, calmly, Emily, why are you mad at Nina?"

"I'm not," she replied.

"That's so not true," Nina said, still sniffling.

"Okay. I am," Emily admitted. "But only kind of."

"Okay, good," I said. "That was good. But you still didn't say why you're mad, Em. *Calmly.*"

Emily took a deep breath. "She had this secret friendship with Zac. She knew it would bug me. That's why she kept it secret. And she was right. It bugs me.

And it bugs me even more because she kept it a big secret."

"I'm right here," Nina said. "You can say my name and tell it to *me*."

"Fine," Emily said slowly. "With all the stuff going on with my parents, it just feels bad that you didn't tell me that you and Zac were texting and Facebooking and stuff."

Nina got off her bed and sat on Emily's. "Listen, Em. I heart you and would never do anything to bust up our friendship or make things weird between you and Zac."

Emily just blew her nose.

"Girls, you fix this or I'll never talk to either one of you again. Ever," I said. "We can't be a threesome if two of us are mad. Now fix it!"

"It's not like this can just be fixed, Claire! It's not like presto: everything's better because *you* say we have to make up." Emily said. Was she annoyed at me now?

"Don't get on Claire's case because you're mad at *me*," Nina said.

Great.

"Listen, I don't want to get in the middle here," I said. "It's probably better if you guys work this out yourselves. But you do need to work it out. We can't go camping with you two mad at each other."

No response from either of them. "I'll leave you to it," I said. I headed out of the bunk.

Another problem with three is that you can end up in the middle. And being caught in the middle is almost as bad as being left out.

CHAPTER 4

I walked away from Emily and Nina's argument, mad at both of them for arguing and mad at myself for getting in the middle of it. As the screen door slammed behind me, I heard the tinkle of the bells following.

The bells on the bunk door were for me. Sometimes I sleepwalk. Yes, it's weird, but I'm used to it. The bells were supposed to let my counselors know if I started the zombie trot out of the bunk in the middle of the night.

In all the years I've been coming to camp, it's only happened twice. The first time was when I was in the youngest group, the Hummingbirds. I was only seven and it was my first year at camp, so I was homesick and getting used to sleeping in a bunk with a lot of people.

It was about three in the morning, and there were no bells on the door back then. My counselor, Arianna, heard me leave and followed me. She said later that after she called my name and I didn't respond, she was scared to wake me. Instead, she just walked behind me and made sure I didn't get hurt. I walked to the flagpole and stood there for a while before heading back.

The next sleepwalking incident was last year when I was a Sparrow. I got out of bed and pulled down my stack of mail. I sat on the floor and started putting letters in different piles. As Sparrows, our camp job was to sort mail, so it wasn't as strange as it sounds. Somehow, I went back to bed, but the next morning, after seeing my piles of mail, I remembered that I was sorting camp mail in my dream.

My dad sleepwalks at home sometimes, so I'm not completely freaked out that I sleepwalk too. But it kind of bothers me. Add it to the list of things I was having mixed feelings about, right after Emily's teasing.

Emily and Nina knew about the sleepwalking. So did Mac, who was in my bunk last year. I had no idea what Zoe and MJ knew. We hadn't talked about it. I was definitely hoping to get through this summer without the zombie thing creeping up again.

I didn't even know why I was thinking so much about sleepwalking as I made my way to the Main House. Daydreaming, I practically ran into Bick, a girl from the Songbirds, the group above ours.

"Sorry! Sorry!" I said as I grazed Bick's arm.

"No prob," she said. "Check this out, Claire, I just got an email from my friend at Camp Winona. They saw a bear on their camping trip to Alpine Woods. A bear, Claire! Can you believe it? I would have freaked!"

"We saw one on our hike last year in Acadia, but from really far away. It was awesome," I said.

"My friend says they stayed in their tents and made a lot of noise and the bear walked away," Bick said.

"I would love to see a bear again, but not *that* close!" I exclaimed.

"Didn't your group already do its hiking trip?" Bick asked.

"Nope. Leaving tomorrow," I said.

"Make sure you have something to jingle. Like rocks in a can or something."

"I'm sure the counselors have figured everything out," I said.

"True. Have a great time! Rocks. In. A. Can," she said and walked away.

"Thanks for spooking me, Bick!" I shouted. Just what a sleepwalking camper wants to think about: bears near the campsite.

I made a mental note for my camping guide.

RAFTING TRIP TIP #2: Be prepared for wild animals near the campsite. Think about bringing loud objects to scare away bears (like rocks in a can).

CHAPTER 5

The next morning, we had to get up before the usual wake-up bugle, so our counselors, Susannah and Astrid, went around gently telling everyone it was time to get up. I maybe closed my eyes again for a nanosecond and before I knew it, Emily had scooted from her bed and started bouncing on mine, up and down and up and down.

"Gran-o-la. Gran-o-la. Wake up, wake up, wake up! Rise and shine, Earth Goddess!" She started pulling my arms. "Up, up, up! Time for the best trip of the summer. Up, up, up!"

I pulled my pillow over my head. "Go away. Go bother other vegan princesses."

"There are none! You are it!" she cried. "Don't make me call for backup!"

I pulled the covers on top of the pillow, which was already over my head.

"C'mon, Zoe, help me get her up," Emily called.

"Let little Clairey have a few more minutes," Zoe said.

"I love you, Zo," I said sleepily.

"If you're not going to help drag her out of bed, I'll have to work twice as hard," Emily said and sat down gently on my legs.

"I'm up, I'm up," I said as I kicked both her and the covers off of me. "Now, leave me alone, you little hedgehog."

"Hedgehog? That's a new one. Who calls one of their best friends a hedgehog?" Emily asked.

"Hedgie, hedgie, hedgie. Now go away," I said.

It took me a while to get moving. And by the time I was ready, almost everyone was already headed to breakfast. Emily was sticking around, waiting for me. I wondered if she was avoiding Nina. They still seemed pretty mad at each other.

Emily and I left the bunk together. As the door closed behind me, I had an idea.

I walked back in. "Ems, grab the step stool from the closet," I said.

"Aye aye, Nature Captain."

She brought the stool over, and I pulled it toward the door. I climbed up and took down the jingle bells.

"In case there are bears," I explained.

She laughed. Was it funny?

CHAPTER 6

We made it to the river by van. After yesterday's fight between Emily and Nina, I thought it might be a good idea if we all paired with other people on the trip. It made me think of my third rafting tip.

RAFTING TRIP TIP #3: Make sure that everyone who's going is prepared to work as a team.

They said that they had made up, and they even sat next to each other in the van, but there was definitely a chill between the two of them.

Why not spend some time with Zoe, MJ, or girls from other bunks? I thought. Normally, Emily and Nina would freak if I suggested it, but I was pretty sure that they might be thinking about the same thing.

We got out of our van at a calm spot along the river. "Listen, girls," I said, about to tell them that I thought we should mix it up.

"Hold up, Clairey," Emily said. "Nina and I were talking in the van and we decided that we should all be on different boats on this trip."

"What?" I asked. Even though that was what I was going to say, I felt like I was getting dumped.

"Is that okay with you, Claire Bear?" Nina said in a soft voice.

"Yeah, sure," I said. "I just wish you had included me in the decision-making. I was sitting right behind the two of you."

"Don't be mad, Claire. We kind of thought it would be good to be with other people, and it wouldn't be fair if either of us was with you," Nina said.

"No worries," I said. I was upset, but I didn't want them to know it. "Yesterday, Zoe and MJ asked me to go with them. So I'll do that."

I found Zoe and MJ and asked them if they wanted one more in their whitewater raft.

"I thought you were going to be with Nina and Emily," Zoe said.

"We decided to switch things up," I said fake cheerfully. I was still annoyed, though I wasn't exactly sure why. Maybe because it was those two making a decision for me.

But Zoe made me feel better. "Cool. We'd love to have you!" she said.

"Mac asked if she could come in our boat too, so we just have to make sure that there's room for four," MJ said.

Mac? Urg. Mac was totally annoying. If I was a goody two shoes, she was a goody two shoes on steroids—like a goody sixteen shoes. She was in our bunk last year and a total pain. I always got the feeling she was trying to make herself look good, instead of just being herself. I *did not* want to spend my time going down the river with Mac. But I guess my choices were limited.

The counselors said that four in a raft was fine, and they assigned us to our guide, Colton, a big, blond guy who greeted us cheerfully.

"Hey, campers!" Colton said. "We're going to have a good time riding the tide."

"Have you been doing this a long time?" I asked, thinking that only a rookie could be that excited.

"Four years," he answered. "And every day is better than the last!"

"So, this is totally safe, right?" MJ asked.

"I've never lost a sailor. Yet!" he said. "It's a short ride downstream. It's pretty gentle. Now, who wants to ride in the front of the raft?"

"Is it extra bumpy or extra dangerous?" Zoe asked.

Colton laughed. "I won't let it be dangerous," he said in a kind of macho way. "It's maybe a teeny bit more bumpy than the regular ride. Someone's gotta sit in front. Any volunteers?"

"I nominate Claire to do it. She's our nature gal," Mac said.

I rolled my eyes. "Thanks, Mac, always ready to volunteer someone else for something," I said.

"Okay, Claire. Are you up for it?" Colton asked. "It'll be a fun adventure."

It didn't sound too bad. Plus, if I were in a boat with Nina and Emily, I knew Emily would be the one to go for it. So, being with these guys gave me a different opportunity. Also, I couldn't imagine that the Kennebec River was going to be too tough a ride.

"Yeah, I'll do it. But we can take turns, Mac, if you want to go too." I was smiling to myself. I knew that Mac would hate it. But since she volunteered me, I thought it would only be fair to volunteer her as well.

"No, that's okay, Claire. I'll let you have all the fun," Mac said.

Colton then took me around the raft and showed me my spot, right near the bow. "You just have to remember that as we hit a rapid, you keep paddling through it," he said.

"Got it!"

We all put on our life jackets. Mac, MJ, Zoe, Colton, and I climbed into the raft, and I sat down in front. I noticed that in boats with three campers, no one was alone in the front like me. Then I spied Nina and Emily arguing about something as they each got into their rafts. *Three minus one, minus one, minus one.*

When I turned around to ask Colton why no one else was in the front of a boat, it was too late. He was already shoving us off.

The water was calm for the first few minutes. I was paddling lightly as we floated along slowly enough that I could enjoy the passing sights. I saw a turkey vulture (or maybe it was a hawk), a heron, and some deer. I had just started getting comfortable when I felt the first bump. It was sort of how my mattress had felt that morning when Emily was bouncing on it. Not a big deal, but I had the feeling that more was coming.

About a nanosecond later, the roller coaster started. We dipped into some whitewater, and everything started rushing by. Colton was right; being in the front was fun! Then things slowed down again.

Colton yelled, "Is everything all right up front, Claire?"

"Yep. I love it!" I replied.

My words were barely out of my mouth when a giant whitewater splash banged into me. My eyes burned, and suddenly it was a lot less fun than it had been. I paddled quickly, like Colton told me to. We cruised into a calmer

area and drifted for a few minutes. At that point, I was ready to leave the front of the boat. But maybe the back wasn't any better.

"You still okay, Claire?" Mac asked.

Was she trying to be thoughtful or stick it to me? It didn't matter, I was fine—it wasn't the best, but I was fine.

Until I wasn't.

CHAPTER 7

We had two more crests and then things totally calmed down again. I returned to watching the wildlife at the edges of the river. I think that's how it happened. My mind started to wander. Then *bang*—water in my face again. My eye stung, so I lifted my hand to rub it. *Bad idea.* One-handed, I couldn't hang on to the paddle when we hit the next big splash. *Whoosh!* I was out of the boat and drinking water. I had my life jacket on, so I popped right up. But the river pulled me downstream along with the rafts. It happened too fast for me to be

completely terrified, but I was pretty scared. I heard people shouting at me, but the rush of the whitewater was loud, and I couldn't hear what they were telling me to do.

I went through the next bit of whitewater, being turned around and around. I popped up and saw someone reaching an orange oar out to me. I didn't even think about who it was. I just wanted to grab it and be back in someone's boat.

I grabbed the paddle. Nina, who is totally afraid of water, was on the other end, reaching over the side of her raft to pull me in. If I could have shouted, I would have screamed, "Don't fall in!"

Astrid, our counselor, who was in Nina's raft, started helping her pull me in. I got a little stuck on the side of the boat, but the two of them grabbed me and hoisted me onto the raft.

"Claire! Are you okay?" Nina shouted.

I was shivering and still wasn't able to form words. I nodded.

Astrid had a poncho on, and she pulled it off and threw it over my head. Their guide said, "Just get to the middle of the raft to balance us and we'll take you the rest of the way. Now, Astrid, you have to get back to your spot and paddle!"

Nina kept looking over and asking if I was okay.

"That. Was." I paused. "Super. Scary."

"Oh, sweetie," Nina said, looking at me and forgetting to paddle herself.

"Thank you for saving me," I chattered.

Once I warmed up a little, I started to recover. Though being at the front of the roller coaster was fun for a while, I definitely liked the middle of the boat better!

I kept scouting down the river, looking for my raft and MJ, Zoe, Mac, and Colton. I finally saw them right before our last bit of whitewater. Zoe and MJ looked back a bunch of times. Mac was concentrating on rowing and was probably glad that I had disappeared!

We finally finished the ride and landed on the bank at a calm part of the river. We all hopped out and Nina, Astrid, and the rest of the girls from the boat took turns giving me hugs and telling me how brave I was.

"Neens, you saved me, even though you were probably terrified!" I said.

"I didn't think about being scared. I thought about *you* being scared," she said.

Zoe, MJ, and Mac all rushed over. "What happened?!" Zoe asked.

"One minute you were there, then you were out. It was crazy!" MJ exclaimed.

"I'm so sorry I suggested you go up front!" Mac said. "It's all my fault!"

"It was actually a good adventure. Really, really scary though!"

Colton walked over and gave me a high-five. "That was on me, Claire. I've never lost a rider before. I went into that last wave at a funny angle. Forgive me."

"Were you going to come back for me?" I asked.

"I saw that you got into another boat. The rapids here won't seriously injure you—all that would happen is you'd get scraped up," he explained. "If someone comes off a boat, we usually pick them up in calmer waters. Of course, you didn't know that. Sorry about that."

A few minutes later, Emily walked over with the rest of the girls from her raft.

"What's up, what's up, what's up, girls!" she said. "That was fun! Right?"

"Fun? You think falling out of a raft is fun?" I asked, annoyed.

"What? What are you talking about? Who fell out?" Emily replied.

"Well, Claire—" Nina started to say.

"Claire what?" Emily snapped, sounding like there was still frost between the two of them.

"Claire fell out of her boat," Nina said.

"*What?!*" Emily shouted.

"And Neens and Astrid saved me!" I said.

"Nina hates the water. How could she save you?"

I explained what happened.

"Good going, Neens!" Emily said, breaking through some of the ice. Emily, who is not a hugger, gave me one. "You okay?"

I nodded.

"We can start calling you Whitewater," she said. "New nickname."

RAFTING TRIP TIP #4: Don't fall out of the raft! If you do, you might get tossed around a bit, but hopefully someone will be there to save you!

CHAPTER 8

We stopped for lunch and then started our hike. I was ready for something much, *much* less exciting than the raft ride! I was feeling a little like this whole trip had gotten off on the wrong hiking boot. I was hoping that we weren't cursed!

Zoe, MJ, and I were in the middle of the pack, hiking together. We kept hanging out after rafting.

After about a half hour and five fully sung camp songs, MJ said, "So when do we get to the rest stop?"

"What rest stop? We're in the woods," I replied.

"No, I mean, I asked Angus and Lars where I could go to the bathroom on the hike and Angus said, 'At the rest stop,'" MJ explained.

"Um, MJ?" I said. "Our counselors were totally teasing you. There is no rest stop. There's the woods."

"Ew. No way!" Zoe yelped. "Ew."

"It's not a big deal," I said. "You just find a place behind some bushes and you squat."

"Not a big deal to you. You're the Camping Goddess. I go to actual buildings when I'm on vacation. We don't squat to pee. Ew! I don't even have any toilet paper," MJ said.

I laughed. "If you really have to go, then squatting's kind of your only option. And I have tissues," I said, producing a package from my pack.

"Well, I *really* have to go," MJ said.

"Me too," Zoe added. "Right now, behind a tree doesn't sound so bad."

"I'll go with you guys. We just need to tell someone that we're going off the trail," I said.

We found Lars, Astrid's best friend/maybe boyfriend, and told him that we were going off for a few minutes. "To the rest stop," MJ said, acting mad.

Lars laughed. "You knew we were kidding, right? You knew there wouldn't be a McDonald's on the trail with a bathroom, right?"

MJ pouted. "I thought there'd be a park ranger station or something."

"Anyway, Lars, we'll catch up," I said.

RAFTING TRIP TIP #5: If nature calls and you need to go off the trail, make sure you go with friends and that someone in your group knows where you are going. Also, it's a good idea to bring tissues.

I led Zoe and MJ to a little area off the path with high grass and some trees.

"We really have to go out here?" Zoe asked.

"This is a good spot. I'll guard for you," I said. "Go down there. I'll stay up here in case someone comes."

They walked a little farther down a small hill and then in opposite directions. They were hidden enough so no one could see them. But, of course, while I was waiting, all of their talk about having to go finally got to me. After a little while, I followed them into the high grass. I couldn't see out, so I hoped that no one could see in!

Just my luck, right in the middle of peeing, I heard big steps coming toward us. Scary, big, bear-like steps.

CHAPTER 9

The footsteps totally scared me. I didn't even have to look. I knew what it was. I could just feel it. A bear.

I was never wrong about these things when I was camping. But how could this happen on a day when I fell off a raft? Bad luck was definitely following me. This *was* a cursed camping trip!

I sprang into action mode. I shouted down the hill to Zoe and MJ. "Don't panic, but I think a bear is coming. Try to make as much noise as possible. Don't run. We can scare it." I started walking toward them.

I got out my bells from my pocket and started shaking them. I jingled and jingled, but the footsteps were coming closer. I really thought the bells would work, but the steps were louder and louder. The hair on my arm was standing on end as I shout-sang "Home on the Range," trying to scare it away.

I could feel that it was a few steps away. I knew you weren't supposed to run, but I was about to take off down the hill.

Then I heard it.

"Hi, there. Are you from a camp group?" a voice called out.

I exhaled and stopped shaking the bells. The bear wasn't a bear after all. It was two boys from Eagle Rock who had gotten off the trail. What are the odds that they would find us right as we were peeing? Probably better odds than a bear finding us, I guess! They walked toward me.

Zoe and MJ were still screaming. I waved to them. "It's okay, guys. It's some boys. Not a bear!"

The boys cracked up. "You thought we were a bear?" the taller one said. "Hilarious!"

My whole body was still tense from thinking that a bear was coming, but I had to laugh. "That's why I was shaking my bells, and we were all screaming. We thought we'd be able to scare off a bear." I told them about hearing about bears from another camper right before we left for our trip.

They introduced themselves: Grant and Josh. They were in our age group at Eagle Rock. Somehow, they lost their group on the hike.

Grant's version was: "Josh was pointing out a rabbit that he thought was hurt. We went to help it, and just as we got there, it hopped away."

"Hilarious!" I said, the same way they said it to me about a bear closing in.

They laughed. MJ and Zoe joined us.

"How did you guys get off the trail?" Josh asked.

We all looked at each other.

"We had to pee," MJ said finally.

Totally embarrassing. Of course the boys laughed.

"How could your group go on without you guys?" Zoe asked. "Won't they be worried? Won't they send someone back for you?"

"Well, I'm the nature lover in my bunk, so the counselors kind of know that I wander a little bit when I'm outdoors," Josh said.

"Once you saw that the rabbit was okay, couldn't you catch up to your group?" MJ asked.

Grant turned red. "We figured we might as well, you know, pee. We were already in tall grass and away from the group." MJ, Zoe, and I cracked up.

"Looks like we're all even," I said. "Anyway, our group is just ahead. We haven't been off the trail for that long."

"Long enough to get attacked by a bear," Josh said.

I grinned. "True that."

RAFTING TRIP TIP #6: If you come across other hikers/ campers, it's fun to include them in your journey.

CHAPTER 10

We started walking to catch up with the rest of the Blue Jays. Josh and Grant had no idea how far away they were from the Eagle Rock boys, so they came with us.

We finally made it to the back of the Camp Mon Mon line of hikers. Lars was bringing up the rear, keeping an eye out for us.

"Look what we found!" I said as we caught up to him.

"I told you to leave the animals in their own environments," Lars said, looking at Josh and Grant.

"Funny," Josh said. They introduced themselves.

"You can hike with us. I think your group is at the same campsite. Meantime, if I can get any bars on my phone, I'll call Eagle Rock. They might actually be worried about you," Lars said.

As we continued to walk on the trail, Josh walked next to me. I pointed out lots of plants to him, while he showed me different birds.

"You seem to know the names of absolutely everything," Josh said.

"I love being in nature, seeing different things and knowing what they are," I said.

He smiled at me.

"This might be my last year at Eagle Rock because I want to do an Outward Bound wilderness program," he said.

"That would be so cool. My favorite part of camp is the hiking and canoeing. The more outdoorsy stuff," I said.

"I want to go out to Colorado and rock climb. Or raft," Josh said.

"I've had enough of rafting for a while," I said. Then I told him about falling out of the boat.

"I wonder what I'd do if that happened to me," he said. "Do you ever think about how you'd push yourself if you were all alone in the wilderness?"

"I've thought about it, but I like to camp with other people. Part of what I like about camping is sharing it with my friends. Like, when you found us this afternoon, it wouldn't have been nearly as funny if I hadn't been with my friends."

Plus, I realized, I really couldn't be alone in the wilderness with my sleepwalking. But I certainly didn't tell him that.

"Maybe guys are different that way," Josh said. "I like all my friends at camp, but I don't mind hanging out by myself, either."

"I don't mind being alone. I just don't think I'd have as much fun camping and hiking alone," I said.

Josh stopped on the trail and pointed to a plant. "I know that one. That's a Virginia creeper," he said. He went over for a closer look, bending down and reaching forward to touch some leaves.

I took a step toward him. "Stop! Josh!"

He looked up. "What?"

"You shouldn't touch that. I think it's poison ivy," I said quietly.

"No, it isn't," he argued. "It's a Virginia creeper. We just saw some earlier and our counselor, Paul, identified it for us."

"This plant has three leaves," I said. "What's the rhyme about poison ivy? 'If there's three, then leave it be?'"

"This has five leaves—like a Virginia creeper." He looked at his hands, turning them over and over, as if bumps and blotches would have appeared already if it were poison ivy.

"Um. It just looks like five, because those two are really part of that one. I would back away from it if I were you," I said.

"There wouldn't be poison ivy by the side of a trail, right?" Josh asked.

"Sure?" I said, trying to be nice, though I really wasn't sure why there *wouldn't* be poison ivy along a trail in the wilderness.

Josh must have had the same thought.

"Argh! I'm such an idiot!" he shouted. "I shouldn't have touched it at all. At least I didn't give it to you like a bouquet."

I laughed. "Maybe you'll wanna do that Outward Bound thing with some friends after all."

"Very funny!" Josh grinned at me.

"I'm just kidding you," I said, smiling. "Don't worry.

I have a whole bunch of allergy and itch creams if you need them."

RAFTING TRIP TIP #7: If it's three, let it be. Stay away from plants you aren't sure you recognize, or you could end up with poison ivy, poison oak, or poison sumac.

CHAPTER 11

Josh and Grant met up with their group once we hiked to the campsite. I would have to wait until the end-of-the-year barbecue to find out whether Josh ended up with poison ivy!

We pitched our tents right after dinner. I ended up in a tent with Amarillis from bunk 12B, Sophie from bunk 13, and Astrid. It was still light out at eight o'clock when we were done putting up the tents.

As we were getting ready for the evening campfire, Nina and Emily started squabbling again. Apparently, during the hike, Emily gave Nina a flat tire. That is, she stepped on the back of Nina's boot. They argued and each ended up hiking with other people. I heard both sides of the story and just wanted their fight to be over with!

I sat down and heard them arguing right behind me.

"You deliberately sprayed me when you were putting on the insect repellent," Emily said.

"Do you realize how ridiculous you sound? Of course I didn't do it on purpose," Nina replied. "Just like you didn't try to give me a flat tire on purpose."

"I didn't. I told you I didn't," Emily said.

"You guys have to stop this. We're here to have fun. Not to fight. Now sit!" I commanded.

"Fine. I'll sit here," Emily said and plopped down next to me.

"She's being such a pain," Nina said, crossing her arms and rolling her eyes.

"Sit! There's a spot on my other side," I said. "I'm not letting you guys ruin the campfire for me or for each other."

They both pouted. And it was awfully quiet on our side of the circle.

After the counselors built the fire, they passed out the ingredients for s'mores. I was going to have the vegan version, which meant different chocolate and marshmallows. Astrid told me that they couldn't find graham crackers without honey, which was okay with me. When it comes to sweets, I'll make some vegan exceptions.

Emily turned to Lars, who was handing out the graham crackers.

"I'm going to have vegan s'mores to be just like Whitewater," she announced.

"I don't understand what you mean by Whitewater," Lars said.

I rolled my eyes. "I told you that Whitewater was not a nickname that would work. Give it up," I said.

"What would you like, Emily?" Lars said, confused.

"I'm going to have what Claire is having. Vegan s'mores. In solidarity," she said.

"That's so sweet, Em," I said.

"I will too," Nina piped in.

"You guys are the best," I said. At least they were still on the same page about something.

The counselors decided that our camping trip was a great setting to tell us ghost stories. So a few of them got up in front of the fire one by one, each trying to outdo the others with the scariness of their stories.

Susannah went first, grabbing the flashlight and putting it under her chin, making her look totally spooky. "When I was a little girl," she said, "a voice called to me from the top of the staircase every day." She continued, "The voice would try to make bets with me. It would say,

'Bet you a penny that you can't hop on one leg for thirty seconds,' or 'Bet you can't throw a ball up and down fifty times.' I would stare as hard as I could at the top of the landing, but no one was there.

"As I got older, maybe I was about six, the voice said, 'I want you to jump rope twenty times.' I knew that was something I could do. I got the jump rope and was going to do it when the voice demanded, 'I want you to bet your life.' I freaked! I ran out of the house so fast—I think it's the fastest I've ever run in my entire life! For years after that, I didn't hear the voice.

"Then, when I was around twelve, I was sitting on the staircase with my younger brother. We were putting our shoes on. Out of the blue, my brother, Luke, asked, 'Did a voice from upstairs ever make bets with you?' I freaked out and told him that it had. 'Did it ever ask you to bet your life?' he then asked. Just as he asked, a tennis ball started rolling down the stairs from out of nowhere. We darted out of the house and were scared for life!"

"Scary!" Nina exclaimed and moved closer to me.

"Do you think it's true?" I asked her.

Before I got an answer, Angus, one of our head counselors, got up. Because he's so tall, his face, lit by the flashlight, looked kind of like it was hanging in midair. Talk about creepy.

He started his story. "When I was a lad in Australia, we lived in a house in the country. In the middle of nowhere."

"I love the way he says *nowhere* like he's saying *no wear*," Emily whispered.

Nina rolled her eyes.

"I would go to sleep in my room and I would feel this weird pressure on my forehead when I put my head on the pillow. I felt it almost every night. I was little, so I didn't know that you weren't supposed to feel that. But

then we would visit relatives or friends and sleep over, and I wouldn't feel the same force on my head.

"When I was eleven, we got a cat. Boots was what we called him. Boots liked to stay in my room, and he would sometimes be there when I got ready for bed. The first night that Boots was there at nighttime, he went screeching out of my room the second I felt the pressure on my head. The next night, I brought the cat in and closed the door. This time, Boots chased himself around the room when I felt the force on my head. I was pretty sure that there was a ghost in my room. But I didn't think my family would believe me. So I never told anyone.

"A few years later, when I was fourteen, an older man and his daughter came by the house. They knocked on the door and said that they used to live there. They asked if they could take a tour. They walked all around and my mom invited them to stay for lemonade and cake. While they were sitting around, the daughter, who was about eighteen years old, announced that when she was living in the house, she thought that, for sure, there was a ghost who lived with her. Everyone laughed, except me. And Boots!

"I asked, 'Why did you think there was a ghost?' She pointed to her forehead—to the exact spot where I had felt the pressure—and said that when she was going to bed, there was a force that settled on her, right above her eyebrow. She got used to it, but she was sure that she had been living with a ghost. I pointed to the exact same spot on my own head.

"'We have the same ghost!' I shouted. 'We have the same ghost!' I grabbed Boots and yelled, 'Just ask kitty!'

"The girl's eyes got wide. 'My dog used to bark whenever he was in my room at bedtime!'"

Angus waved the flashlight right at his forehead and we all jumped.

"Scary stuff!" Emily exclaimed.

"I don't know how I'm going to sleep!" I said to Emily and Nina.

"You don't think that this will make you sleepwalk, do you?" Nina asked quietly.

"I hadn't even thought of it, until you just said something," I said.

Emily leaned in. "You wanna sleep in my tent? I can ask Lucy to switch with you."

"You guys don't need to worry. I'll be fine. I've heard ghost stories before," I said.

"But on a day when you got knocked out of a raft?" Nina questioned.

"And on a day when you thought you saw a bear?" Emily added.

"You guys are making me seem like I'm losing it. I'll be fine," I insisted. They looked at each other.

"You know the bells that you brought? The ones from our bunk?" Emily said.

"Yes. I have them." I pulled them out of my pocket.

Nina took them and twisted the elastic band they were on. "Hold this. I'll be right back," she said and rushed toward her tent.

"It's so sweet that you guys are worried," I said, and I mussed Emily's hair.

"You never let anyone worry about you, Whitewater. You're so tough," she said.

"You do know that the nickname is never going to stick, right?" I said with a shake of my head.

"Yeah, I kind of realized it as I said it this time. On to the next," Emily said.

"Thankfully," I said.

Nina came back with an elastic beaded anklet that I made her two years ago. "I can weave the bells into this. That way, you can put it on your foot, and you'll jingle if you wander out of your tent."

It took her about five minutes, but Nina was able

to fashion the bracelet into bell jewelry for me to wear to sleep.

"You guys are the best!" I said and hugged each of them. As I walked over and grabbed my stuff to wash up and brush my teeth, it occurred to me that they had stopped fighting. At least for now.

I got back to my tent and saw that all my tent-mates had gotten into their sleeping bags with their faces completely covered. *Weird. How could they be asleep so quickly?* I was definitely spooked.

As I started to get into my sleeping bag, the two other campers yelled, "Surprise!" It was Nina and Emily!

"Claire Bear, we wanted to make sure that you were okay tonight," Emily said.

"Especially after a day when you fell into the river and got scared by an almost-bear," Nina added.

Even though they had been mad at each other, they figured out a way to help me out.

"What about Amarillis and Sophie?" I asked.

"We muscled them out!" Emily exclaimed, showing her bicep.

We all giggled. I got into my sleeping bag, nestled in between theirs.

Nina propped herself on one elbow and whispered, "You guys don't think all of that ghost story stuff is real, do you?"

"Do you mean in general or do you mean Susannah's and Angus's stories?" I asked.

"Both, I guess," she answered.

"I think Angus's was totally fake. He totally sold it though. The only one whose story might be true is Susannah's," I said.

Emily giggled. "I thought the opposite. Angus, true. The rest fake!"

"Did either of you ever have anything freaky happen to you like any of that?" I asked.

"Well, you know," Nina whispered, "at a friend's birthday party, there was a palm reader."

"Really? What did she say?" I asked.

"That I would make great friends at camp," she said, grinning.

I smiled. "That's not exactly a mystery."

"And save someone from whitewater!" she added.

"*LOL*," I replied. Nina giggled.

"So, do you believe in spirits?" Emily asked.

"Kind of. I don't want to say that they're not there," Nina said.

I sometimes thought that when I sleepwalked, there was something spirit-y about it. Maybe when I become a counselor, I could creep the campers out by telling sleepwalking stories!

We stayed up late talking, until there was no avoiding falling asleep. I didn't think I'd sleepwalk, but I was a little nervous as I drifted off.

I woke up in the middle of the night. Thankfully, I was still in my sleeping bag in my tent. Hooray! I looked around and repositioned myself, tinkling the bells.

Emily bolted up in her sleeping bag. "Did you hear that?"

"What?" I whispered.

"I heard bells," she said.

"Is Claire okay?" Nina asked sleepily.

"Go back to sleep. I didn't hear anything." I smiled to myself.

RAFTING TRIP TIP #8: If you get scared by ghost stories, keep friends around you.

CHAPTER 12

The next day, after we hiked some more, we piled into our vans to go back to Mon Mon. When I hopped in, Emily and Nina were already sitting next to each other.

Two together. One extra.

"Sit with us, Claire. We'll make room," Nina said. She and Emily scooted in opposite directions so that I could sit between them.

"We're a threesome again," Emily announced.

"Even though we had a fight, we never stopped being a threesome," Nina said.

"We weren't two . . ." Emily said, pointing at Nina and me, ". . . plus one?" She pointed to herself.

I laughed. "You know, before this trip, I was thinking that sometimes I'm the extra." I had never said it out loud to anyone.

"I've thought that about myself too! Especially when we're doing yucky water sports and you two do the girl-guide bonding thing," Nina said.

"And when you two were working so hard on the play, I felt the same way," Emily said.

We all laughed. It was funny that we all had the same feelings.

"But we're better as three," I said.

"Triplets!" Emily shouted.

"Now, that's a nickname that could stick," I said with a smile.

ABOUT THE AUTHOR

Wendy L. Brandes, an attorney, is quite familiar with the excitement, fun, adventure, trials, and tribulations of summer camp. Initially a reluctant camper, she attended summer camp in the Adirondacks for four years and sent both her son and her daughter to camp in Maine. A published legal writer, Wendy notes that she has had far more fun writing this summer camp series and reliving her days as a camper. She lives in Manhattan with her husband, her children, and her dog, Louie, a black lab.

ABOUT THE ILLUSTRATOR

Eleonora Lorenzet lives and works in Osnago, a small village in northern Italy. After studying foreign languages in high school with the hopes of traveling the world, she attended the School of Comics of Milan. Eleonora has always wanted to be an artist, but if she wasn't an illustrator, she says she'd be a rock star. Or a witch. Or a character from the manga series *Sailor Moon*.

GLOSSARY

collapse (kuh-LAPS)—to fall apart or fall down suddenly

confident (KON-fi-duhnt)—sure of oneself

hoist (HOIST)—to raise

infirmary (in-FUR-mur-ee)—a place where sick people receive care

ingredient (in-GREE-dee-uhnt)—an item used to make something else

insecure (in-si-KYOOR)—anxious and not confident

organically (or-GAN-ic-lee)—something that happens naturally

pharmacy (FAR-muh-see)—a place that sells medicine

solidarity (sol-uh-DA-ruh-tee)—an agreement among a group of people that they will work together to achieve their goal

vegan (VEE-guhn)—a vegetarian who does not eat any animal or dairy products

GATHER 'ROUND THE CAMPFIRE

1. For most of the story, Nina and Emily are upset with each other. Are their feelings justified? Why or why not?

2. Some of the girls don't like Mac. Do you like her? Use specific examples from the story to support your answer.

3. Do you think Claire is a confident person or an insecure person overall? Use examples from the story to explain your answer.

GRAB A PEN AND PAPER

1. Claire writes wilderness tips for the camping guide. Write three more tips to add to the list and explain how they relate to the story.

2. What if Claire, MJ, and Zoe had come across a bear instead of Grant and Josh? Write what might have happened.

3. Emily and Nina put Claire in the middle of their fight. Write about a time when you were put in the middle of a fight. Compare your situation with the situation in the book.

DON'T HEAD HOME YET! THERE'S LOTS MORE TO DO AT SUMMER CAMP!

MJ has a secret, and she's not sure what to do. When she met her new bunkmate, Zoe, she couldn't stop thinking her fantastic new friend seemed familiar. Then she realized why — Zoe is the daughter of the lead singer of MJ's favorite band! She's dying to tell someone but figures Zoe wants to keep it quiet. But what if she only told her brother? Telling one person won't create much trouble, right?

Emily is known for saying exactly what's on her mind. But there's one thing she's not willing to talk about—her parents' constant fighting. Happier than ever to escape to camp, she distracts herself by pulling pranks, each bigger than the last. But when a prank goes too far, her counselor is ready to send her packing. Will Emily get to stay at camp, safely away from the drama at home, or will her pranking problem get her sent home early?

Nina wears two labels: boy crazy and camp drama star. But this summer things are different. First she finds herself interested in Emily's brother, Zac. But everyone knows that brothers are off-limits. Then instead of getting a lead in the camp musical, she gets a smaller part that normally goes to a boy! Much to Nina's surprise, her summer is about shedding her labels and discovering what she's capable of.

CHECK OUT MORE ADVENTURES!